MINI MANNERS MATTER

Written and Illustrated by

LAURA ANN BINGHAM

For my three monsters, Jason, Justin and Jacob.
You make me proud everyday.

Mini Manners Matter
Text and Illustrations copyright © 2021 by Laura Ann Bingham

Library of Congress Control Number: 2021900045
ISBN: 978-1-7363146-0-9

Printed in the United States
10 9 8 7 6 5 4 3 2 1

Busy Bee Books
5020 Clark Road Suite 105
Sarasota, FL 34233
powerlifeproject.com

WELCOME MY FRIENDS, SIT BACK AND ENJOY,

THIS FUN LITTLE TALE OF A GIRL AND A BOY.

FLIP THROUGH THE PAGES AND SOON YOU WILL SEE,

WHAT GOOD LITTLE MONSTERS THEY TURNED OUT TO BE.

Mini monsters are girls and boys.
In monster families they bring such joy.

But there are times
they can run **WILD**.
Forget their manners
like any child.

Milo and Macy
are monster twins.
Forgetting their manners
is where trouble begins.

Often they could be a mess...

His scruffy hair.

Her juice stained dress.

And their mother
she would say,
"Minis...you can't
look that way."

Mini Manners Matter

Comb your hair.

Show the world
that you do care.
Wash up each and
every day.
Then you may go
out and play.

Now, minis tracked in mud
and messed up floors.

They ran through halls
and slammed the doors.

They did not mean to be so rude.
They had a careless attitude.

And again their mom would say,
"Minis, you can't act that way."

Mini Manners Matter

Indoors we should settle down.
Be thoughtful how we move around.
Pick up messes, make things neat.
When called to dinner take a seat.

Though it may not be what you had planned...
ask if you may lend a hand.

At the table they would sit.
Not so still and fidget a bit.

Milo's napkin fell to the floor,
Across the table...
          he grabbed for more.

Then their dad would calmly say,
"Minis, please don't act that way."

Mini Manners Matter

At the table, you must sit still.
Pass the plate, try not to spill.
Keep your napkin on your lap.
Sit up tall and try not to nap.

Table manners you will learn.
Respect of others you will earn.

After dinner,
     help to clean.
Please then follow your
     night time routine.

Brush your teeth,
     put your PJs on...

In the morning,
    they would wake.

Roll out of bed,
    which they forgot to make.

Thump downstairs and
    cry for food.

Their mouths wide opened as they chewed.

Out the door and running late.
They missed the bus that came at eight.

All the family turned to say,
"You should not be late today."

Mini Manners Matter

When it's morning, rise and shine.
You must always be on time.
You should neatly make your bed.
Prepare yourself and plan ahead.
Set out your clothes,
the night before.
Then you will be ready
to head out the door.

Their mother drove them both to school.
She reminded them of the golden rule,
"Mind your manners and be kind.
If you do, the more friends you will find."

They got to class before the bell
and things were going pretty well.
They neatly put their things away
and followed the other children
on the floor to play.

It seemed they wanted everything,
the doll, the truck and the bouncy spring.
The other children got upset.
Then something happened they would not soon forget.

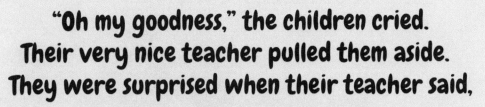

"Oh my goodness," the children cried.
Their very nice teacher pulled them aside.
They were surprised when their teacher said,

"I believe you've been misled.
Here in school we share the toys.
They belong to ALL the girls and boys.

Minis, it is not okay for boys and girls to act this way."

Mini Manners Matter

They did not want to make them sad,
or ever make their teacher mad.

They thought about what their teacher said...

and finally a lightbulb went off in their heads.

Their mother told them to be kind
and if they did the more friends they would find.

They now truly understood...
how minding your manners was very good!

Mini Manners Matter!

Mini Manners Matter!

Mini Manners Matter!

Mini
Manners
Matter!

Mini Manners Matter!

Mini Manners Matter!

Make your own Mini Monster!